LADYBIRD BOOKS, INC.
Auburn, Maine 04210 U.S.A.

LADYBIRD BOOKS, LTD.
Loughborough, Leicestershire, England

Printed in U.S.A.

Busy Beavers

CARLA the CARPENTER

By Cathy East Dubowski

Illustrated by John Speirs

Ladybird Books

Carla Beaver is a carpenter. Ever since she was little, Carla has loved wood. She can make anything from wood, and she does very careful work.

The Kanga twins need new beds. Carla measures carefully. She saws the wood in a nice straight line.

Then Carla puts all the pieces of wood together with glue and nails and screws. The wood fits together just right.

The twins try out their new beds.
Mrs. Kanga is pleased. "Thank goodness
your beds pass the test!" she says.

Next, Carla puts the finishing touches on Mr. and Mrs. Squirrel's new kitchen cabinets and drawers—all fifty-seven of them!

"They're beautiful!" says Mrs. Squirrel.

"Now we have room for all the nuts we collect!" says Mr. Squirrel.

At Town Park, Carla finishes building some new playground equipment. She makes it high enough to be fun, and strong enough to be safe.

"It's so nice, I would like to play here myself!" she says proudly.

Then Carla sits on a swing and has her lunch. Guess what she does on her lunch break. She carves some wood!

Carla's biggest project is the new house she's building. The house will have to last a long, long time. Every bit of it must be perfect.

Carla checks the building plans very carefully. She measures everything twice. She makes sure every part goes where it should.

Carla makes sure that the windows
are straight.

She puts up doors, and makes sure the hinges work without squeaking.

Carla makes sure the kitchen cabinets
won't fall off the walls!

At last the house is finished. Carla
steps back to take a look…
"Oh, no!" she cries. Everything
looks wrong!

How did the doors
turn out so tall and
skinny?

Carla can't even
reach the windows!

"Oh, dear. Look at the kitchen!"
says Carla. "I can't believe it!
I followed the plans carefully."

"How could I have gotten things so wrong?"

There's only one thing
to do. Carla calls the new
owners. "I'm afraid there's a
problem with the house,"
she says. "Can you come
over and take a look?"

Carla sits down on her tool box to wait.
How will she ever explain what happened?
    Then she hears someone exclaim, "Oh,
look, dear—isn't it beautiful?"
    "Yes, dear. It's the most wonderful house
I've ever seen!"

Carla looks around. No wonder the house looks so tall—the new owners are giraffes! Carla sighs with relief. Everything *is* just perfect after all.

Here are some of Carla's favorite tools.

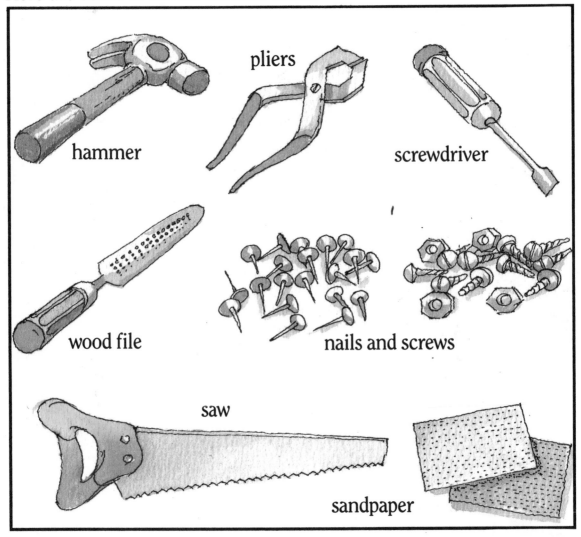

hammer

pliers

screwdriver

wood file

nails and screws

saw

sandpaper